ZOOM AWAY

by TIM WYNNE-JONES

pictures by ERIC BEDDOWS

A Laura Geringer Book
An Imprint of HarperCollins*Publishers*

Zoom Away. Text copyright © 1985 by Tim Wynne-Jones. Illustrations copyright © 1985 by Ken Nutt. First published in Canada by Douglas & McIntyre Ltd., Vancouver, British Columbia. Printed in the U.S.A. All rights reserved. Library of Congress Cataloging-in-Publication Data Wynne-Jones, Tim.   Zoom away / by Tim Wynne-Jones ; pictures by Eric Beddows. p. cm.   "A Laura Geringer book."   Sequel to: Zoom at sea.   Summary: Zoom and his friend Maria search at the North Pole for elusive Uncle Roy.   ISBN 0-06-022962-4.   ISBN 0-06-022963-2 (lib. bdg.)   [1. Cats—Fiction. 2. North Pole—Fiction.]   I. Beddows, Eric, date, ill. II. Title. PZ7.W993Zp 1993   [E]—dc20 92-41171 CIP AC
1 2 3 4 5 6 7 8 9 10 ❖ First American Edition, 1993

ZOOM WAS KNITTING SOMETHING WARM. Outside, it was summer. All the other cats were in their light summer coats, chasing butterflies and rolling in the grass. But Zoom had other plans. His friend Maria had called.

"Dress warmly," she had said.

He knocked three times on her big front door and waited.

"No time to lose," she said as she let him in. She was dressed in the fluffiest coat Zoom had ever seen.

"I received a letter from your uncle, Captain Roy, some months ago. He was going to sail to the North Pole. He hasn't written since. Will you come with me and search for him in the High Arctic?"

"Yes," said Zoom.

"Good," said Maria.

Maria showed Zoom a map of the North Pole. Zoom put on his backpack and they started up the wide staircase in the front hall.

Zoom had never been upstairs in Maria's house before. The staircase was very long and steep. The air grew cold. There were little hills of snow in the corners of each step. The windows on the landing were prickly with ice, and long icicles hung like teeth from the archway.

The hall was carpeted with snow. Zoom put on his ping-pong paddle snowshoes.

From a dark room Zoom heard the howling of wolves.
"Owwwwwww."
Maria suggested they sing a song so as not to be afraid.
Zoom followed her down corridor after corridor, from room to room. There was deep snow everywhere.

At last Maria stopped and checked her astrolabe.

"This will be a good place for lunch," she said.

They brushed the snow off two comfy chairs. Zoom placed tin cups on a frozen end table, and Maria took out a thermos bottle and filled each cup with tomato soup.

Not long after lunch they came to a narrow hall which led to a little room. There was a low wooden door in the little room with the words "Northwest Passage" carved over it.

Zoom could hear the wind whistling and thumping against the other side.

He put on his goggles. Maria opened the door.

Oh, how the wind howled—louder and more ferocious than a pack of wolves.

Zoom lit his lantern. The doorway was very small. Too small for Maria.

"I'll have to find a different way," she said. "I'll meet you on the other side."

Zoom entered a tunnel of ice. It was very dark and very cold. Soon his paws were numb. Frost tugged at his whiskers.

I hope it isn't much farther, he thought.

Then he saw the light up ahead—the end of the tunnel.

Zoom scampered out into the light. Ice was everywhere, glistening and glaring in the bright sun. The air smelled like the sea.

"Yahoo!" he cried. "The North Pole."

Zoom tied on his skates.

"Whee!" he shouted. "I'm skating on the Arctic Sea."

Round and round the wind twirled him. Gulls circled, laughing. A noisy colony of grebes crowded in close to watch. Seals barked and clapped. Zoom didn't feel cold anymore.

But after a while he got tired. Out of breath, he clambered to the top of a frozen hill. He took out his spyglass to look around. There was a ship stuck in the ice.

"*The Catship,*" he read on the bow. It was Uncle Roy's boat!

Zoom hurried over. The ship looked deserted.
"Hello," called Zoom. "Anyone on board?"
There was no answer.

In the galley there was a note on the table.

To whom it may concern:

My crew and I have boarded a passing iceberg and are heading south. We have lots of food and water and are in a merry mood. Be sure to give my love to Maria and my trusty nephew Zoom if you should meet them in your travels.

Yours affectionately,
Captain Roy

P.S. I'll be back for The Catship *when the ice melts.*
P.P.S. She's loaded deep with cargo bound for warmer climes!

Beside the note was a captain's whistle.

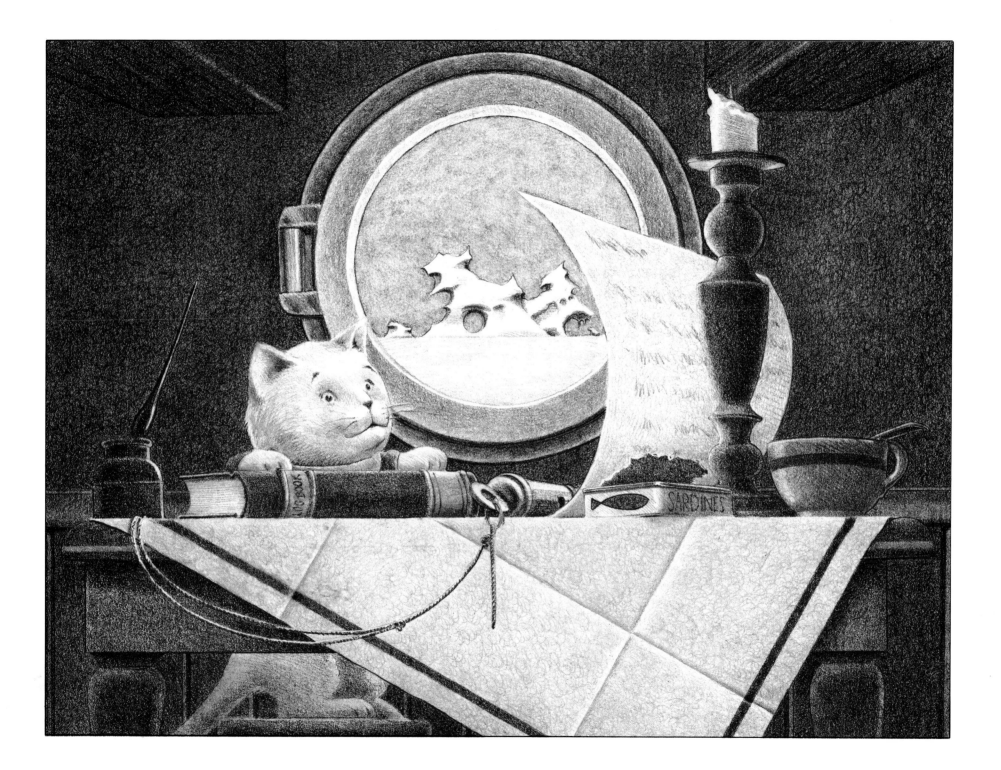

Zoom put the whistle around his neck. He looked through a porthole out at the snow. He felt sad. He had hoped to see his uncle.

Thud, thud, thud! Footsteps. There was someone on the deck above.

It was Maria!

"Am I glad to see you!" said Zoom.

Maria had made a sled out of two oars and some sailcloth. Zoom climbed on before telling her all about the note and the iceberg and Uncle Roy's escape.

"Warmer climes," said Zoom. "Imagine that!"

Maria tucked him in nice and cozy. He yawned.

"It's all downhill from here," she said.

Zoom drifted happily off to sleep with the arctic sun beaming down on his face.

When Zoom woke up, he was curled in the wing chair in front of the fireplace in Maria's sitting room. Maria was asleep on the couch.

Zoom licked his paws and snuggled down again. He had been having a nice dream about traveling with Maria and Uncle Roy to somewhere warm. Where, he wondered. And when would he see the brave captain?

He closed his eyes.

He hoped it would not be too long.

For Xan, Maddy, and Lewis
—T.W.J.

For Clarence, my dad
—E.B.